THE DAY WE RODE THE RAINBOW

JODI F. MAYS
ILLUSTRATOR: M. J. REINHARDT

ISBN: Softcover   978-1-4691-8646-7
           Hardcover   978-1-4691-8647-4

For more information and to order
additional copies of this book,contact:
www.thedaywerodetherainbow.com
Email:werodetherainbow@aol.com

Xlibris Corporation
www.Xlibris.com

Book meets US Consumer Product Safety Commission Requirements
The Harris Group -'The Day We Rode the Rainbow'
Printed and Bound in Guangzhou, China
Lot 1001-5000 April, 2014
10 8 6 4 2

Author J. F. Mays was born in Boston, MA. She moved with her family to Austria at a young age. She obtained her business and marketing degree in Europe and is currently living in California and Europe.

M. J. Reinhardt is an Austrian illustrator. She enhances the mood and fantasy of young readers by using rich, happy colors and a whimsical approach making new worlds come alive through her imaginative and enchanting illustrations.

. . .

"Treasure of a book with engrossing, whimsical illustrations, great life messages and descriptive prose ... enchanting, magical page-size illustrations ... diverse and colorful characters in this story lend themselves ideally for a perfect read-aloud during story time and/or to act out in a class performance ... to include every child—Butterflies, Dancing Flowers, The Whirling Wind, and many more" ...
—Educator Edith Paulsen

"Appealing, descriptive narrative with delightful, bright, and cheerful illustrations—this enchanting story is a valid reason for parents and children to lay down the electronic gadgets and enjoy a fun bedtime story together ... appeals to a wide range of young readers. Rich illustrations and a magical tale of seven good-hearted rascals provide ample material for an interactive parent-child discussion about values and social skills that should not be forgotten."
—Prof. Marcus Tobishek

"Children can identify with each of the characters, whether reading the book under supervision, or on their own—and cull confidence from the fact that others share their feelings, fears, and foibles in a fun and playful way."
—Dr. D. Covi

Love
to the best Mom
in the world and
to my pride and joy
Morgan

Daisy and Lily were twins. The two butterflies had beautiful, colorful wings. They looked exactly alike except that one had pink polka dots and the other had blue polka dots.

Today they were very excited!

Their friend Spruce Jr. would be here any minute and other friends were coming too. They pushed their acorn stools back under the mushroom table and cleared off their breakfast plates as fast as they could.

BUTTER & FLAKES

MILK

They were going to play together the whole day.

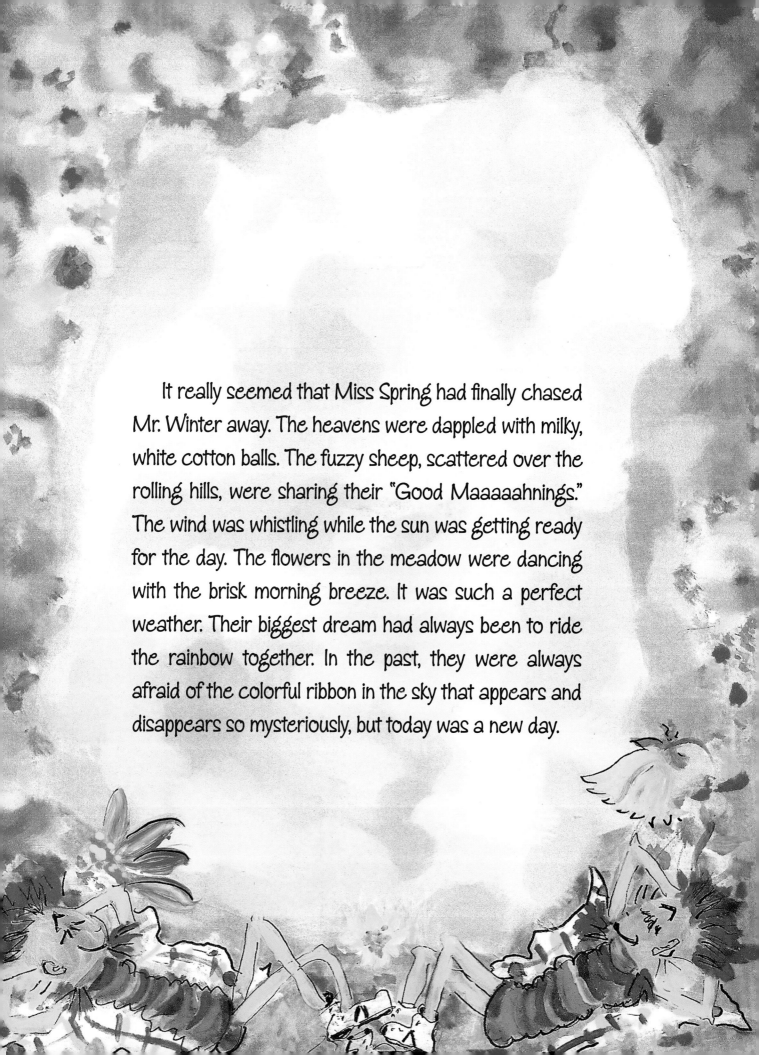

It really seemed that Miss Spring had finally chased
Mr. Winter away. The heavens were dappled with milky,
white cotton balls. The fuzzy sheep, scattered over the
rolling hills, were sharing their "Good Maaaaahnings."
The wind was whistling while the sun was getting ready
for the day. The flowers in the meadow were dancing
with the brisk morning breeze. It was such a perfect
weather. Their biggest dream had always been to ride
the rainbow together. In the past, they were always
afraid of the colorful ribbon in the sky that appears and
disappears so mysteriously, but today was a new day.

dreaming
dreaming
dreaming

Oh! What fun they were going to have!

The twins had just finished making their beds when they heard the flitter-flatter of fluttering wings. "They're here, they're here!" they shouted. Yahooooooo!

There they were. All their friends were coming around the big oak tree, right on time. It was easy to see them with their radiant colorful wings. Spruce Jr.'s gold-tipped wings looked so majestic, as if he had dipped his wing tips into a pot of gold.

Then there was Little Koa, always, trying to catch up. The cast on his leg surely did not help things, but he never complained and never asked for help.

"Good Morning," the twins shouted in unison. "Let's go to the lake to greet the new little ducklings!"

"Hey, you two—it's too early for that," said bossy Spruce Jr. "We'll wake them up. I think we should let Salvio have a turn to decide what to do. What do *you* want to do, Salvio?"

Salvio put on his thinking cap while he looked spellbound at the twinkle of the fields covered with morning dew. The sun was just popping her head out and peeking over the hills. The sparkle of the dew droplets, covering the grass and colorful flowers, turned the meadow into a field of diamonds

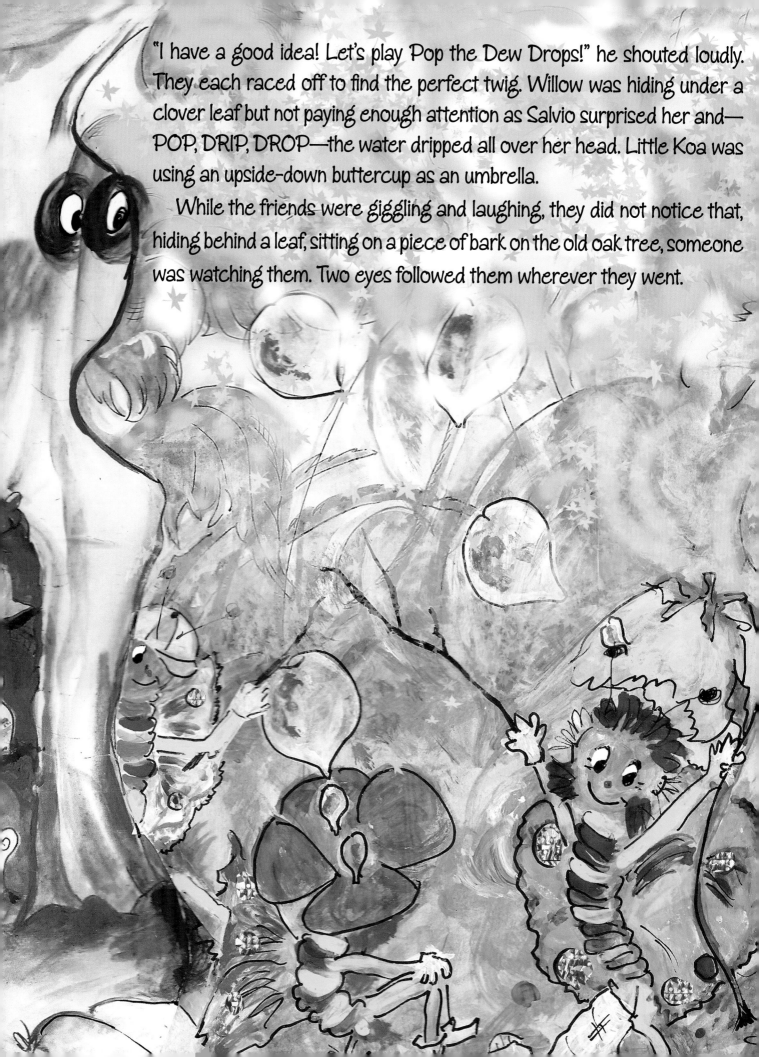

"I have a good idea! Let's play Pop the Dew Drops!" he shouted loudly. They each raced off to find the perfect twig. Willow was hiding under a clover leaf but not paying enough attention as Salvio surprised her and— POP, DRIP, DROP—the water dripped all over her head. Little Koa was using an upside-down buttercup as an umbrella.

While the friends were giggling and laughing, they did not notice that, hiding behind a leaf, sitting on a piece of bark on the old oak tree, someone was watching them. Two eyes followed them wherever they went.

It was Basil, another butterfly—a butterfly with gray, drab-colored wings. Basil was very sad, and teardrops rolled down his cheeks. His only real friend, the Whirling Wind, whispered to him, "Why don't you go play with them?" Wiping away his tears, Basil answered, "Look at them and look at me. They'll never want to play with me."

Why don't you go play with them?

From his secret hiding place, poor Basil continued watching them as well as the two little farmer children finishing their morning chores next door. Farmer Boy was feeding the pigs in the pigsty, and his sister was surrounded by clucking hens eating the corn that she threw from her bucket. Basil loved watching the children's adventures.

The two children dashed in and out of the bales of hay. They pretended to climb the highest mountains, to sail across vast oceans with pirates, to explore the dense jungle, to camp out with bears, fight mean dragons, and even have picnics on the moon—and all that without ever leaving their backyard.

Basil decided to fly to his favorite weeping willow and rest on one of the drooping branches to get a closer look at the children's exciting adventure they had planned for the day. It was getting windier and windier, and he was swinging back and forth on the branch.

Oh, good, Basil thought, *the two children are going to paint.* They had already set up their paint pots and brushes on the picnic table. All of a sudden, there was a strong gust of wind, and Basil could not hold on to his branch.

The strong gust pushed Basil off his branch right into their paint pots. He tumbled and tossed, topsy-turvy, and all around. When he regained his balance, he flew away.

Basil screamed to his friend, the Whirling Wind, "Hey, best buddy pal, what are you doing to me?" He received no answer and sat down on the tree stump to wipe the paint out of his eyes. And then he saw it.

He took a second look at himself and could not believe his eyes. He was beautiful. His wings were all the colors of the rainbow.

At last, he felt, he was the same as the others and could play with the rest of the butterflies.

He flew as fast as he could to find them. They were playing Hide-and-Seek. He flew right up to them and said proudly. "Hi, my name is Basil. Can I play too?"

"Sure," Willow answered. "The more the merrier."

After Daisy and Lily saved Little Koa, who got stuck in a spider web, the seven butterflies played and played.

They played Catch Me If You Can. They visited the new ducklings, had a picnic on green moss, followed some huge animal tracks, and tickled each other with daisies.

They were having so much fun that they did not notice that the dark gray clouds were filling up the sky until the first raindrops started to fall.

They quickly picked up their picnic basket and dashed back home. As Basil was trailing them, he suddenly noticed colorful raindrops started to fall.

Why did it have to rain today?"

"Oh no! The rain is washing off my color," he cried to himself. He quickly hid behind the leaf on the old oak tree. He could not hold back his tears.

"That was the most fun I have ever had and that rain had to ruin it.

Slowly the pitter-patter of the afternoon showers stopped, and Basil heard his name,

"Basil, wherrrrrrre aaaaaaaare youuuuuuu?"

Spruce Jr. yelled.

Basil was afraid to come out with his dull, drab-colored wings, so he just explained honestly to his friends from behind the leaf exactly what happened and that the real Basil is different from them. He apologized again for misleading them and expected them to leave. But they did not go. Basil waited a bit longer. But they did not go.

It was then that Willow explained to Basil, "It doesn't matter to us that you are different. Just think . . . there is no one like you around here, and that's really cool. More important is that you are so much fun. We would miss not having you play with us."

"Please, please come along," Willow and Little Koa begged.
"We want to play Follow the Leader and ride the rainbow.
With you leading the way, we won't be afraid of getting lost.

Hurry, hurry before it disappears."

Dreams really do come true!

FOLLOW ME

Slowly, Basil came out from behind his hiding place and shrieked gleefully, "Can I really be the leader?" And off they flew to finally ride the rainbow together . . .

What do YOU think Basil looked like after he fell into the paint pots?

Color me!